Harry walked slowly over to the table. "It'll be strange . . . someone living in the house. Someone from another country." He looked down at the eggs. "I wonder what she'll be like?"

Mum looked thoughtful. "I don't really mind where she comes from," she said. "I just hope she's got some common sense." She bashed the top of one of the eggs with a spoon. "That's what I need. A nice down-to-earth girl . . ."

# YOUNG CORGI BOOKS

Young Corgi books are perfect when you are looking for great books to read on your own. They are full of exciting stories and entertaining pictures and can be tackled with confidence. Whatever your interests you'll find something in Young Corgi to suit you: from ponies to football, from families to ghosts. There are funny books, scary books, spine-tingling stories and mysterious ones. The books are written by some of the most famous and popular of today's children's authors, and by some of the best new talents, too.

Whether you read one chapter a night, or devour the whole book in one sitting, you'll love Young Corgi books. The more you read,

# Astrid
## the Au Pair from
## Outer Space

# For Kate, Charlotte and Freddie

ASTRID, THE AU PAIR FROM OUTER SPACE
A YOUNG CORGI BOOK : 0 552 54616 X

PRINTING HISTORY
Young Corgi edition published 1999

3 5 7 9 10 8 6 4 2

Copyright © 1999, Emily Smith
Illustrations copyright © 1999, Tim Archbold

Set in 16/20pt Bembo Schoolbook
by Phoenix Typesetting, Ilkley, West Yorkshire

Young Corgi Books are published by Transworld Publishers Ltd,
61–63 Uxbridge Road, London W5 5SA,
in Australia by Transworld Publishers,
c/o Random House Australia Pty Ltd,
20 Alfred Street, Milsons Point, NSW 2061,
in New Zealand by Transworld Publishers,
c/o Random House New Zealand,
18 Poland Road, Glenfield, Auckland,
and in South Africa by Transworld Publishers,
c/o Random House (Pty) Ltd,
Endulini, 5a Jubilee Road, Parktown 2193.

Printed and bound in Great Britain by
Cox & Wyman Ltd, Reading, Berkshire.

# Astrid,
## the
## au pair
## from
# OUTER
# SPACE

### Emily Smith
### Illustrated by Tim Archbold

## YOUNG CORGI BOOKS

# The Beginning

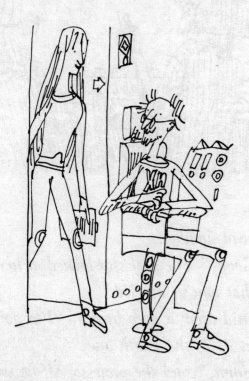

Astrid slid open the panel and stepped into the study.

"Ah, Astrid!" Professor Xn turned from his console. "Come about your research project, have you?"

Astrid nodded.

"Good!" The professor looked at her. "Tell me what you've decided."

Astrid drew a deep breath. "I'm going for Project 492, the Earth one."

"Hmm," said the professor. If he was surprised he didn't show it. Swinging back to the console, he tapped a few keys on the keyboard.

"Here we are, Project 492." He read from the screen. "The study of home life in a typical Earth family, with particular reference to young humans."

He leant back on his couch and looked at her. His face was serious.

"Studying a family," he said slowly, "is a big project. It's not like working on . . . sea-water samples or plant forms."

Astrid nodded. "Yes, I know."

"It would really be best if you studied the family from the inside. Live with them, even."

"I agree." Astrid smiled. "And I've decided on the best way to do it."

"Oh?" He looked at her, eyebrows raised. "And how's that?"

I'm going to go as . . . as an 'au pair'."

Professor Xn's face changed.

A look came into it —
a look which she had
never seen before.

It was a look of
complete and utter
surprise.

"A what?" he said.

9

# Chapter One

"A what?"

Five hundred light years away, in an untidy kitchen in west London, Harry Henderson was staring at his mother.

"An 'au pair'," said Mum.

"Well, I don't want one!" cried Harry. "I don't like 'em!" He frowned. "What is an 'au pair', anyway?"

"An 'au pair'," said Mum, "is someone who comes from another country to live with you in your house."

"Live with us?" said Harry.

"Yes," said Mum.

"In our house?"

"Yes," said Mum.

"Here?" said Harry.

"Yes," said Mum.

Harry was silent for a minute. "But what for?"

"Well, it works like this," said Mum, getting out some eggcups for tea. "The au pair gets to learn English and earn some money. And I get some help in the house, and with you and Fred. Er . . . mostly Fred, of course!" she added hastily.

"Fed!!" said Fred happily, at the sound of his name. He was busy stuffing the head of a toy clown into a plastic teapot.

"We've got the spare room," said

Mum. "And it will mean I can go back to work part-time."

Harry frowned.

It looked as if Mum had worked it all out.

"But no-one at school has an au pair," he said in a low voice.

Harry hated to be different from other people. What if Rod Beevor – the school bully-boy – found out? Rod liked it when people were different from other people. What would Rod say about Harry Henderson having an au pair? Harry shuddered to think of it . . .

"You're wrong!" said Mum. "Someone at school does have an au pair."

Harry looked at her. "Who?"

"Josie Phelps," said Mum.

"Great!" Harry rolled his eyes. "Josie Phelps! Well, that's OK then . . . not!"

Mum put the eggs and toast on the table. "Come on, guys!"

Harry walked slowly over to the table. "It'll be strange . . . someone living in the house. Someone from another country." He looked down at the eggs. "I wonder what she'll be like?"

Mum looked thoughtful. "I don't really mind where she comes from," she said. "I just hope she's got some common sense." She bashed the top of one of the eggs with a spoon. "That's what I need. A nice down-to-earth girl . . ."

# Chapter Two

Harry talked to Josie in break. He chose
a moment when Rod Beevor was
picking on a little kid (there were plenty
of those to choose from).

"Josie?" he started.

"Mmmmm?" said Josie. She was
chewing something.

"Mum says you've got an 'au pair'."

Josie nodded. "Mmmmm," she said, jaws working.

"Well, what's it like?" asked Harry. "What's she like?"

Josie swallowed, and thought. "Well, she makes this strange fruit salad with everything cut up tiny, and raisins in it."

Harry waited, but she didn't go on. "And?" he prompted.

"But she does bring nice things back from home," Josie admitted. "Chocolates and stuff."

"But that's just about food!" cried Harry. "What about other things? What's she like?"

Josie gave a shrug. "She's OK."

Harry gave up.

He went over to his friends Luke and Oz.

"What was all that about?" said Luke.

"Au pairs," said Harry shortly.

"Pairs of what?" said Oz.

"Au pairs," said Harry.

"Oh pairs of what?" said Luke.

Harry sighed. "Don't you know what an 'au pair' is?"

"No," said Luke.

"Me neither," said Oz.

There was a silence.

"Well?" said Luke. "What is a 'no pair'?"

Harry sighed again. "I'm sorry, I don't want to go into it right now . . ."

Mum looked at the kitchen clock. "Someone called Elena should be coming soon. In about ten minutes."

"Ten, four, five, three, nine!" cried Fred.

"An au pair?" asked Harry.

Mum nodded.

So it really was happening, thought Harry.

Elena was bang on time.

"Bang on time!" said Mum when the bell went. "Good sign." She looked at him. "You go, Harry!"

"OK." He went to open the door.

There on the doorstep, stood a girl – a very pink girl. She had a pink face, a pink fluffy jersey and tight pink trousers. "'Allo, 'allo!" she cried. "I ham Elena! I ham after being your au pair!"

"Er . . . come in," said Harry.

He led her into the kitchen.

"Good evening, I ham Elena!" cried the girl.

"Hi," said Mum faintly.

"Pinka-pinka-pinka!" said Fred brightly.

Elena turned to him. "And this must be the little Fred!" A frown crossed her face. "'E is very – 'ow you say? – grubby!"

"Yes, er . . . he is a bit," said Mum. "You see, we've just taken him to the park."

"The park?" said Elena.

"Yes, he loves it there," said Mum.

Elena shook her head. "Ah, but these parks are so dirty." Her pink face lit up. "But when you 'ave me here, I will keep 'im at 'ome in the very clean kitchen."

"Er . . . I see," said Mum.

Elena nodded. "Twice a day I clean the kitchen with the antiseptic."

"Gosh!" said Mum feebly.

"And three times on Saturdays and Sundays."

"Ah," said Mum.

"Because I like things to be clean."
There was silence.

And Mum drew a deep breath . . .

★ ★ ★

Everyone was rather quiet after Elena
had gone.

"I hope I did the right thing," said
Mum, after a bit.

"You did, Mum," said Harry. "She
would have been a nightmare!"

"Yes," said Mum. "But a clean
nightmare." She sighed. "Oh dear,
perhaps this whole au pair idea is a
mistake. Perhaps—"

Suddenly the bell went again.

"Who can that be?" said Mum miserably.

Harry walked to the door, and threw it open.

There on the threshold stood a girl – a girl with long golden hair, and the greenest green eyes Harry had ever seen. She was smiling.

"Hello," she said. "I'm Astrid."

# Chapter Three

"Where did you say you were from?" said Mum.

"Antalusia," said Astrid.

"Ah!" said Mum. "Antalusia. Yes. Antalusia."

She was frowning to herself. She clearly didn't have a clue where it was, any more than Harry had.

"Well, you're a long way from home!" she said at last.

"Yes," said Astrid. "I'm a very long way from home."

"But your English is very good!" said Mum warmly.

Astrid nodded. "We Antalusians are

good at languages. We learn quickly. But I won't have the words for things we don't have at home."

"Well, there can't be so many of those!" said Mum in an encouraging tone.

And Astrid smiled . . .

Harry watched her. There was something strange about Astrid – but also something nice.

And he could tell that Mum liked her.

He glanced at Fred. He was busy chewing a plastic dinosaur – but his eyes were on the green-eyed girl.

"We ought to tell you a bit about us."
Mum looked at Harry. "In fact, you do
that, Harry, while I ring the agency
from the hall."

"Me?" said Harry. "Us? But I
don't—"

But Mum had gone. Harry met
Astrid's gaze. She looked at him, waiting.

He drew a deep breath. "Well, there's
really not much to say," he muttered.
"Apart from Dad being away in the
Gulf at the moment, working. I mean,
we're very sort of ordinary . . ."

"Ordinary?" said Astrid.

"Yes," said Harry sadly.

"But how . . . wonderful!" Astrid cried.
"That's just exactly what I want! An
ordinary family — with an ordinary
mother."

They heard Mum laugh in the hall. "I
guess I'm that!" she called.

Astrid looked at Harry. "And you,
Harry — an ordinary boy!"

Harry looked back at her. She so wanted him to be ordinary, it was difficult to refuse. "Yes," he said with a shrug. "I guess I'm ordinary."

Astrid looked over at Fred. "And an ordinary little girl."

There was silence. The only sound was Mum talking on the phone.

"No," said Harry.

Astrid raised her eyebrows. "Fred's not ordinary?"

"Fred's not a girl!" said Harry.

Fred took the dinosaur out of his mouth, and met Astrid's astonished gaze.

"Not a girl?" said Astrid.

"No."

"She's a boy?"

Harry nodded. "She's a . . . I mean, *he*'s a boy." He coughed. "Fred's a boy's name."

Astrid gave a wail of disappointment. "But I told the agency I wanted one of each!" She looked at him with her large green eyes. "Are you sure he's a boy?"

"Quite sure!" said Harry firmly.

"And what about you? Are you sure you're—"

"*Quite* sure," said Harry, even more firmly.

"Oh, dear!" cried Astrid. "I don't know! You seem such a perfect family – but I did want a girl!"

"You mean—" Harry's heart gave a jump. "You might not come to us after all? Just because we haven't got a girl?"

There was silence for a moment. And then Astrid said, "But you know girls, don't you? You have friends that are girls?"

Harry considered. "Well, yes, I suppose so."

"Then you could ask them here!" Astrid cried in triumph. "And I could talk to them!"

Their eyes met.

This is it, thought Harry. This is the deal.

It was either girls – and Astrid.

Or it was no girls – and no Astrid.

He made up his mind.

"OK," he said.

Just then Mum came back. "All right, you two!" she said. "Sorted everything out?"

Astrid and Harry looked at each other.

And then they both said, "Yes!"

Mum smiled at Fred. "And what do

you say, Fred? What do you say about Astrid?"

Fred took the dinosaur out of his mouth.

Then he put it back again.

Then he took it out again.

Then he gave his verdict. "Like Aglid!" he said.

# Chapter Four

"Is that your stuff?" said Mum.

She looked at the grey oval-shaped thing at Astrid's feet.

"Yes," said Astrid.

"What a smart case!" said Mum.

Astrid's face lit up. "Oh, so you know what it is!" She touched the gleaming oval with her foot. It trundled over the doorstep, into the house.

Mum looked a bit startled but turned to Harry. "You take Astrid up to her room, will you? I'll put the kettle on for tea."

"Sure, Mum!" said Harry eagerly. "Come on, Astrid."

He started up the stairs, and then a thought struck him. What about the case? Maybe he should offer to carry it?

He turned back. Maybe he should – eek!

The thing was gliding noiselessly up the stairs behind them.

He looked at the thing. Then he looked at Astrid. Then he looked at the thing again.

"It's amazing!" he breathed.

"No," said Astrid, turning green eyes on him. "Just a Smart Case, like your mum said."

"A Smar—?" Suddenly Harry clicked. "Oh!" he cried. "Smart, as in clever!"

"Yes," said Astrid. "Of course! Are you telling me you don't have Smart Cases here after all?"

"No." Harry shook his head. "Just ordinary stupid ones."

And he turned and slowly walked up the stairs.

Astrid seemed to like her room. One thing seemed to puzzle her, though — the little jug of flowers that Harry and Fred had picked for her and put in her room.

"Oh!" she cried. "Cut plant parts!" She looked at Harry. "Are these for eating?"

"No," said Harry. "They're just . . . to sort of, look nice."

He was amazed that she was amazed. Gran always seemed so pleased with her little jug of flowers when she stayed.

But Astrid just stood there, gazing at it. Suddenly she clapped her hands "Data log!" she cried.

"Er . . . what?" said Harry.

But it seemed she wasn't talking to him at all. She was talking to the Smart Case. He stared as a panel of the Smart Case opened with a low hum. Inside was a compartment, containing a small black machine. Astrid picked it up, held it in front of the flowers, then murmured something into it.

Then she looked up at him, a strange expression on her face. "Talking of eating . . ." she said slowly. "There was something I wanted to ask you . . ."

"Oh, yes?" said Harry, and for some reason his heart leapt into his mouth. "What?"

"Is it really true that you eat animals?"

There was silence. He looked back at her. "Um . . . well, yes."

Astrid winced, then she nodded. Then she murmured something into her data log.

Suddenly she smiled – a warm big smile, which lit up the whole room.

"So tell me, Harry!" she cried. "When you're not eating animals and putting cut plant parts around the place, what do you like doing?"

Harry let out a deep breath. He knew the answer to that. At least there was something in this whole weird conversation he was sure about. He beamed at her, and said, "Football!"

Her eyes grew big. "Football?" she said. "What's football?"

Harry watched as Astrid kicked the ball against the garden wall. She was good at it. Surprisingly good at it. Kick, hit, bounce. Kick, hit, bounce. Kick, hit, bounce. She could even put a spin on the thing and get it back.

Suddenly he frowned (after all, he was supposed to be teaching her) and stuck a foot out.

Bad move. The ball hit his trainer, and curled high into the air. It came down and bounced several times on the paving between him and Astrid.

She looked at the ball, then him and suddenly her green eyes were alight. "Oh, Harry!" she cried. "I do love your gravity!"

He blinked. "Er . . . thanks," he blurted out finally. "Thanks a lot!"

# Chapter Five

Harry sat in his room zapping alien
Mega Bugs. Nicka-nicka-nicka-nicka –
zap! He had really got the hang of it
now. Nicka-nicka – doiiinggg! Drat,
missed! All the time he was playing he
had the feeling that something was
wrong. He zapped another three, missed
two and suddenly realized what it was.
There was no sound of the vacuum
cleaner.

He frowned. Mum had taken Fred to
the doctor's, and had asked Astrid to
vacuum the front room while she was

gone. So why wasn't she doing it?

He shrugged, and turned back to the game. Well, it was nothing to do with him. He couldn't look after Astrid all the time! He couldn't help it if she was going to get into trouble with Mu— Oh, bother! He got to his feet and stomped down to the front room.

Astrid was hard at work. But she wasn't hoovering. She had got lots of bits of cloth and was stuffing them round the window frames.

Harry stared. "What are you doing?" he said.

"Sealing the windows!" said Astrid.

"Sealing the windows! But . . . but, what for?"

"For the vacuum, of course!" Astrid peered down a crack. "You have to seal any outlets to get a vacuum. Surely you know that?"

"But, um . . . why are you trying to get a vacuum, Astrid?"

Astrid looked at him. "Your mother asked me to vacuum the room. So I am going to do it for her."

There was a determined note in Astrid's voice. Very determined.

Harry went out of the room, his mind whirling. Perhaps you could clean a room by making a vacuum? He couldn't remember anything about it in Science. But perhaps he hadn't been listening when it came up.

The thought of Science led to the thought of Oz. Oz was a bit of a Science whizz . . .

"Yes?" snapped Oz, when he came

to the phone.

"Oz?" Harry said, in a rather wobbly voice. "It's me – Harry." He swallowed. "Oz, what would happen if you made a vacuum in someone's front room?"

"Oh, Harry!" said Oz crossly. "I'm just about to get the Chess Demon's queen on my computer and you pester me with silly questions!"

"Please, Oz!" begged Harry. He glanced down the hall to see Astrid gazing sternly at the door frame.

"Oh, all right!" said Oz. "A vacuum, you say? In a front room?"

"Yes," whispered Harry.

"What sort of house?"

"Well, this sort of house, really."

"Hmmmm," said Oz, thinking.

"Terrace. Bricks and mortar. Well, I think the house would probably just implode."

"Implode?" asked Harry.

"Opposite to explode," explained Oz.

"Ah!" said Harry, spirits rising. "So not too bad then?"

"Exploding inwards, that is," Oz went on.

"Exploding inwards?" squawked Harry.

"Bring the house down, probably," Oz went on. "One or two others in the terrace too, I wouldn't wonder. It might even—"

But Harry didn't hear the rest.

He grabbed Astrid by the arm. "No, no, no!"

"What is it, Harry?" she said, surprised.

"Astrid," he said firmly. "You've got it all wrong."

He led her to the kitchen. He walked to the cupboard. And he pulled out the Hoover.

"Astrid," he said. "Can I introduce you to the vacuum cleaner?"

# Chapter Six

Astrid took an interest in things. She took an interest in interesting things, like football matches and the new laser guns with Mega Bug stick-ons. But she also took an interest in uninteresting things.

Like clothes pegs.

Or soap. Or coat hangers.

Or zips. Or the things Mum stuck in the end of corncobs when they had sweetcorn for tea.

"OK," she ordered, holding her data log up.

"Show me you eating sweetcorn on prongs!"

So Harry showed her him eating sweetcorn on prongs.

He also had to show Astrid him brushing his teeth, and him pedalling his bike. In fact she also got him wobbling

into flower pots, him falling off and him splitting his trousers.

She was always asking questions too. And there was one person in the house who was always pleased to answer Astrid's questions. Fred. Fred loved having someone to tell things to.

One afternoon he gave Astrid a tour of the kitchen.

"Tatoes!" he said, pointing to the vegetable rack with the air of a guide in a stately home. "Big tatoes and little tatoes." He beamed proudly. "Lotsa tatoes."

Harry squinted at the page of his book. He was trying to do his homework.

"And what are these?" said Astrid.

There was a moment's silence. Then Fred said firmly, "Nunions!"

Astrid frowned, and murmured. "Tatoes. Nunions."

Harry shook himself, and read what he had just written. ". . . was invaded by the Nunions." He sighed, crossed out "Nunions", and changed it to "Normans".

Fred had moved on to the fruit bowl now. "And dese," he was saying, "are nanas."

"Nanas," repeated Astrid – and suddenly Harry could bear it no longer.

"Ba-nanas!" he burst out.

They both looked towards him.

"What?" said Astrid.

"Ba-nanas!" said Harry.

"Ba-what?" said Astrid.

"Ba-nanas!" shouted Harry. "Bananas, bananas, bananas!"

Astrid and Fred looked at each other.

"Nanas," whispered Fred.

Astrid held her data log over the

bananas. "Nanas," she murmured. "Also known as ba-nanas."

Harry sighed, and turned back to his history.

Then a thought occurred to him. "Astrid?" he said.

"Yes, Harry?"

"What are bananas in your language?"

"We have no bananas."

"No bananas?"

"No bananas."

Harry frowned. "What about . . . apples, then? What are apples in your language?"

"We don't have apples either," said Astrid.

No apples? No apples? He thought again. "Potatoes, then," he said. "You must have potatoes!"

Astrid shook her head. "We don't!"

Harry stared at her. No potatoes? No mash, no roast, no baked potatoes – no

chips! Imagine living in a country
without potatoes! A no-potato-zone.
Wow! He shook his head. Astrid's
country must be some weird place . . .

Astrid was now at the kitchen drawer,
holding up the can-opener. "And what's
this called, Fred?"
she asked.

Fred thought,
then beamed. "Fing
what you open beans wiv!"

She nodded, and repeated his words.
"Fing what you open beans wiv . . ."

# Chapter Seven

"Spit!" shouted Harry.
    Astrid didn't move.

    "Go on, spit: turn over another card."
    Astrid looked down at the cards
spread out on the floor, and turned over
a six.

Harry started piling cards onto her six, and then suddenly realized she was quite still. She just wasn't playing, even though he could see she had cards to play.

He sat back on his heels. "Come on, Astrid!"

She gave a little shake of the head. "Sorry, Harry," she said. "I'm afraid I don't feel too well."

Harry looked at her. She didn't look well. Her green eyes had gone yellowish, and her skin looked . . . well, green.

"I think I'll go to my room for a bit," said Astrid, standing up.

Harry looked up at her. "Will you be all right?" Astrid nodded. "Yes," she said, "I'll be fine. It's just everything's so different here. It takes time for me to . . . adjust."

She walked stiffly to the door and went out.

Slowly Harry cleared away the cards.

He was worried. Astrid really had looked strange. He decided to go to the kitchen and look for something for her. A treat, that's what you need when you are ill.

Opening the cupboard door, his eyes lit on a can of Coke. That was it! Pouring out a glass, he carried it upstairs. Then he knocked on her door.

"Astrid, can I come in?" he called.

"Yes!" came Astrid's voice through the door.

He walked in — and saw her.

She was sitting on the bed, her Smart Case on the floor beside her — and she was grinning all over her face.

"Oh!" he said. "You're better!"

"Yes!" cried Astrid.

He stared at her. "But how?"

"My Smart Case mixed some medicine for me and it worked!"

He looked down and saw that a compartment in the Smart Case was open. He could just make out rows of tubes of different coloured liquids.

"Wow!" he said.

Astrid grinned happily. "Good, isn't it?"

"Yeah . . ." He looked down at the glass in his hand.

He felt a bit silly about it now.

"I brought you something," he said.

"Oh, thanks!" said Astrid. She took the glass and looked in it. "What is it?"

"Coke!"

"'Coke'?" said Astrid. "What do you mean 'Coke'?"

Harry sighed. "Just Coke."

"What's Coke?"

"Oh, you must know what Coke is!" he said. "Everyone knows what Coke is! It's like . . ." He tried to think of something that everyone knew about. "It's like Mickey Mouse!"

"Mickey Mouse?" said Astrid.

"You know — big round ears!"

"Big round ears?"

Harry stared at her. "You can't not know Mickey Mouse. Everyone on this planet knows Mickey Mouse!"

Astrid looked at him.

She looked at him for a very long time.

And then she said, "Harry, I think it's time to tell you something."

She went out of the room, and came back with his big fat encyclopaedia (Mum had given it to him one birthday, but he also got rollerblades). They sat together on Astrid's bed, and Astrid turned the pages.

She turned past the map of Europe.

She turned past the map of the world.

She turned to the map of the stars.
And there she stopped.
Harry raised his eyes to hers.
"No," he said softly.
"Yes," said Astrid. "I told you I was
from Antalusia, didn't I?" She put her
finger on a spot near a star called
Betelgeuse. "Well, Antalusia's about five
hundred light years away in that
direction."

# Chapter Eight

It's a shock to find you have an alien living in your house. Anyone would find it a shock. Harry found it a shock.

"You're an alien!" he cried.

Astrid nodded.

"You're from outer space!"

Astrid nodded.

"B-b-but you look so much like us!" he said.

Astrid's eyes glimmered. "We aren't all like those little green men in your comics."

"But what—" Harry's mind was racing. "I mean, how did you get here?"

"Usual way!" Astrid gave a shrug. "Spaceship!"

"Spaceship?" He gaped at her. "Where is it?"

Astrid clapped her hands. "BCL-22!" she cried.

They both looked down at the Smart Case. A panel was sliding to one side. In the compartment was a greenish-silvery object on four metallic legs.

It looked a bit like a spaceship. Yes, thought Harry. It could be a spaceship. It definitely could be a spaceship. Except for one thing. It was about fifteen centimetres long. Suddenly he burst out laughing. "You couldn't fit in there!" he cried.

"Well, not like that," agreed Astrid. "But when it's full-size I can."

"Oh, yes?" said Harry, grinning. "And how do you make it full-size?"

She looked puzzled. "The Smart Case, of course."

"The Smart Case? That can make things bigger and smaller?"

"Of course!" said Astrid. "There's no point in a case that can't shrink things, is there? I mean, how do you possibly get everything in?"

"Er – I'm not sure."

Harry put his hands over his eyes. Everything was going too fast for him. The questions crowded his brain. OK, so Astrid

was an alien. But was she a friendly
alien? Was Astrid trying to take over
Earth – or was she just going to make
him beans on toast for tea?

He opened his eyes again. "Astrid?"
he whispered.

"Yes?"

"What are you doing here?"

Astrid smiled at him. "I'm studying!"

He breathed out. This was better.

"Oh, yes? What are you studying?"

She smiled again. "I'm studying you."

"Mum?" said Harry, that evening.

"Mmmm?" Mum was trying to check
some accounts at the kitchen table.

"Did you know Astrid was an alien?"

"An alien?" said Mum vaguely. "Well, yes."

Harry stared at her. "What! You knew Astrid was an alien?"

"Yes, of course!"

He was silent for a bit.

Then he said, "But doesn't it seem a bit strange to you to have an au pair from outer space?"

Mum looked up from her accounts. "Outer space? Harry, what are you talking about? Alien just means from another country, that's all. It doesn't mean Astrid's from outer space!"

"Even so," Harry insisted. "Astrid is from outer space."

"Oh, sweetie!" said Mum. "You've been watching too many Mega Bugs!"

"No, it's not that," said Harry slowly.

Mum shot him a look. "Don't you like Astrid, Harry? I thought you did."

"Yes!" said Harry hastily. "I do! A lot. But . . . but she says she's studying me, and I'm not sure I like that."

Mum turned back to her accounts. "Well, that's what au pairs do – study other countries. It's what it's all about!" She ran a finger down a column. Suddenly she looked up again. "Though, if she is studying you, may I suggest you improve your table manners . . ."

# Chapter Nine

"Owwwwwwwww!"

The cry rang round the house. Harry froze. It sounded like Fred.

"Ow-ow-ow-ow!" came the cry again. It *was* Fred.

Harry leapt to his feet, and pounded up the stairs towards the noise. He found Fred outside Astrid's room, glaring at the Smart Case and rubbing his side. "Fred! What happened, Fred?" he cried.

"Smarcase ouched me!" said Fred indignantly.

"What?"

"Smarcase ouched me!" repeated Fred. "It gave me a bump!"

"I see." Harry relaxed – he could see Fred wasn't seriously hurt. "Well, what were you doing with Smarcase, I mean, the Smart Case?"

Fred shook his head sadly. "Just wanted a ride."

Harry stared at him. "You sat on it?"

Fred nodded. "But it went whoosh, and I falled off."

Harry was aghast. "But you shouldn't have done that, Fred! The Smart Case is high-tech – very, very high-tech! You musn't sit on very high-tech things."

Fred gazed up at him. "High-tech" did not seem to mean much to Fred.

"And anyway, it's not yours."

Fred gazed up at him. "Not yours" did not seem to mean much to Fred either.

"Next time you do that, Smarcase will bite your bottom!"

That did it. Fred did know what "bite your bottom" meant. "Ow-ow-ow!" he cried. "Don't want Smarcase bite my bottom!"

Harry had got used to seeing the Smart Case in the house. But he hadn't bargained on it out. He hadn't bargained on it going shopping. There they were, he and Astrid, just about to go to the shops. And there it was. Lurking at her feet. Looking as if it thought it was coming too . . .

He stared at it in horror. "That's not coming!"

"Of course it is!" said Astrid.

"No way!"

"Yes way!"

"But it'll look so odd!" he cried. "People will stare."

Astrid's eyes flashed. "I need my Smart Case, Harry. To put things in. Or move things. Or . . . or shrink things. In Antalusia you never know when you're going to need your Smart Case. My Great Great Aunt Zapha once left it—"

But Harry wasn't listening. He was thinking.

"Can the Smart Case hang sideways up?" he asked.

"Of course!"

"At sort of . . . hand level?"

"Anywhere."

"And move along?"

"Yes."

"That's it then!" said Harry in triumph. "That's it!"

They set off.

The Smart Case hovered by Astrid's left hand. Anyone looking closely would have seen that she was not actually holding it. But no-one did look closely . . .

Harry quite enjoyed the shopping at first. They looked at

69

some CDs. They bought some vests for Fred. They found Luke a Chicago Bears baseball cap for his birthday. And they went to the health food shop and bought 12 packets of dried bananas.

(Astrid had discovered dried bananas soon after her arrival. They were just a bit like her favourite food on Antalusia, she told Harry. The other Earth food she really liked was swede.)

After that he and Astrid walked to the market to buy some fruit. And there they bumped into Rod Beevor.

# Chapter Ten

Rod Beevor was a bully. Your heart sank just to look at him. He was a bully in school. He was more of a bully out of school. And he was even more of a bully out of school with one of his mates. And today he was with one of his mates . . .

Rod's mate was a tall red-haired boy Harry had never seen before. He and Rod were standing by a big pile of cardboard boxes. Harry put his head down, and tried to walk past without being seen. Not a hope.

"Oooh, look who's here!" he heard Rod shout. "It's little Harry Henderson from school!"

Harry tried to take no notice. Just keep on walking, he said to himself. But as they got closer, Rod noticed Astrid.

"Hey, Harrikins!" he jeered. "I see you're out with your nanny!"

The red-haired boy smirked.

Harry felt his face grow hot. And then he made a mistake. "She's not a nanny!" he said. "She's an au pair."

Rod laughed. "She is too your nanny!" he jeered. "Has she changed your nappy today, Harrikins? Has she made up your bottle?"

The red-haired boy smirked again. And . . . Harry saw red. He put his hands on Rod's chest – and pushed.

Rod fell back against the pile of boxes and the next second there he was, lying on the ground – surrounded by boxes, old bananas and cabbage stalks. Harry gaped at him in horror.

"Strange way to greet a friend," Astrid said in an interested way. "Do you always—?"

He grabbed her arm. "Come on!" he said.

"What? Why?" she said.

"Come on!"

They didn't stop till they got to the little alley which Mum always used as a short cut. Harry just stood there, panting.

"Why have we left the market without our fruit?" asked Astrid. "We need fruit."

"I don't need fruit!" said Harry.

"Well, I'll get it then," said Astrid.

"OK," said Harry, still panting. "OK, you get it. But I'll wait here."

"All right." Astrid nodded. "You stay here with the Smart Case."

Immediately the Smart Case went gliding down to lie at Harry's feet. And Astrid was gone.

Harry stood in the alley and waited. Astrid seemed to be taking a long time.

Maybe she was in a queue. Sometimes you did have to queue a long time at the market. He kicked a stone against a wall. Then he looked at the clouds in the sky. Then he looked at a crack in the pavement. And then he heard a voice.

"Well, hello there, Harrikins."

## Chapter Eleven

He turned. But he knew who it was
even before he looked. Rod Beevor and
the red-haired boy. Harry glanced
around. There was no-one about. And
the pair of them were moving towards
him.

Rod had a grin on his face — not a nice grin. The red-haired boy's eyes were narrowed, as if he was sizing Harry up. Harry began to back against the wall.

"We're coming to get you . . ." called Rod in a sing-song voice.

Harry gulped, looked around again — and then down. And there, by his side, was the Smart Case. The Smart Case! His brain started working furiously. What had Astrid said about the Smart Case? Surely, surely she had said that it moved things. Well, he wanted Rod moved — and quickly! Harry bit his lip. It might do things for Astrid but would it work for him?

Rod was getting nearer, his bunched hand raised high. It was worth a try!

"Smart Case!" Harry gasped. "The boy in the black shoes — move him!"

The effect was amazing. One minute Rod was standing, fist raised. The next minute he was still standing, fist raised – but about four metres higher. He would have been about the same height, if he'd been standing on an elephant. But he wasn't standing on an elephant. He was standing on thin air.

The nasty grin fell from his face, to be replaced by a look of pure horror. When you want to beat someone up, being four centimetres higher is fine. Being four metres higher is not. That's what Rod seemed to be finding anyway.

The red-haired boy looked up at him and gasped. Then he found his voice. "Rod?" he called.

Rod looked down at him, then back up quickly. "Aaaaaargh!" he went.

"What you doin', Rod?" said the red-haired boy.

The only reply Rod gave was "Aaaaargh!"

"Come down, Rod!"

"Aaaaargh!"

There was silence.

The red-haired boy turned to Harry.
He seemed a bit more friendly now.

"Weird!" he said.

Harry nodded.

Together they looked up at Rod. He
seemed less frightened now. He realized
that at least he wasn't going to fall. He
started waving his arms and legs around

but he wasn't going anywhere.

"Get me down!" he shouted.

The red-haired boy glanced around. "I guess we'll need a ladder!" he shouted back.

"Well, get one!"

"OK!" shouted the red-haired boy. "I'll see if I can find one."

He glanced up. "You stay right there!"

He was gone. Harry stood there, frowning. It was good to see Rod stuck up there like that. But perhaps he could make it even better. He had to act fast (people were beginning to stare down the alley). Suddenly he grinned to himself.

"Rod?" he shouted up.

Rod looked down at him. "Yes?"

"If I get you down, will you promise not to bash me?"

A pause, then came the wail. "Yes!"

"And do you promise never to beat me up again?"

"Yes!"

"Or call me stupid names!"

"Yes!"

This was easy.

"Or—"

"Harry!"

It was a very angry voice. He turned and saw a very angry Astrid . . .

Twenty seconds later Rod Beevor was safely back on firm ground. He was unhurt – but surprisingly quiet. Thoughtful, even. He wasn't going to cause any trouble, Harry could see that. Hovering – impossibly – four metres above the world for a few minutes had had a good effect on him. A very good effect . . .

No, Rod wasn't going to be a problem any more. Harry's problem was with someone else.

Harry's problem was with Astrid.

## Chapter Twelve

Back home, there was a row. It was an intergalactic row. Astrid's eyes flashed like lasers, and she kept using a terrible Antalusian word that sounded to Harry's ears like "sink plunger" (though he decided not to tell her this).

Apparently to use someone else's Smart Case without telling them was one of the most terrible things you could do on Antalusia. Fred was delighted with the row.

"Harry been naughty with Smarcase!" he kept crying happily. "Smarcase gonna bite Harry's bum!"

Then, suddenly, the row was over. Intergalactic peace broke out again. But not before Harry had promised two things. Not to use the Smart Case again.

And to get on with asking a girl to tea.

He decided that it had to be Josie. He would have liked to ask Sarah Whitehouse. Sarah Whitehouse had yellow hair, and was the fastest runner in the class. But he felt Josie would understand about au pairs – she wouldn't think them odd. And he was also a bit shy of Sarah . . .

"OK," said Josie, when he asked her. "I'll come." She looked in the bottom of a bag of crisps she was eating. "But why are you asking me?"

Harry swallowed. "Well, it's for Astrid, really. Our au pair. She'd like to . . . er, talk to you."

"Your au pair?" Josie curled her lip. "I'm not sure I want to talk to someone's au pair!"

She really was awful, thought Harry. He wished he'd asked Sarah instead. But it was too late now. He went over to join Oz and Luke.

"What was that about?" said Oz.

"I've just asked Josie Phelps to tea," said Harry.

"What?" said Oz.

"Pardon?" said Luke.

"I've asked Josie Phelps to tea," said Harry.

"Why?" said Oz.

"What for?" said Luke.

"Because she's a girl," said Harry.

Oz and Luke looked at each other.

"Yes?" said Luke.

"And?" said Oz.

Harry sighed. "I really don't feel like going into it right now."

# Chapter Thirteen

Astrid was very excited about Josie coming.

"Josie, Josie, Josie," she murmured to herself, trying to remember the name.

There was a lot of crashing around the kitchen as she made a nice tea. And she kept on thinking of questions, like "Do girls float better than boys?" or "Do girls like Brussels sprouts more than boys?"

Harry felt uneasy. He kept telling himself there was nothing to be uneasy about. Josie would just come, answer Astrid's silly questions, eat a big tea, and go again. What could possibly go wrong?

The first thing to go wrong was Astrid's hair. Usually she wore her long hair loose down her back. But when he walked into the kitchen just before Josie came, he got a shock. Astrid was standing there, her hair sticking out all around her head like a huge dandelion clock.

"Astrid!" Harry cried. "What's happened?"

Astrid patted the huge globe of hair. "Nice, isn't it? We always do it this way in Antalusia for special occasions." She looked at Fred. "You like it, don't you, Fred?"

Fred nodded. "Fat hair!" he said happily.

"Bu – bu—"

And then the bell rang.

"I'll get it!" shouted Harry.

"No, no!" said Astrid grandly. "I will get it!" And she walked to the door.

Josie's face was a picture when her eyes fell on Astrid.

"Does she always look like that?" she hissed to Harry, as they followed the huge round head to the kitchen.

Harry shook his head wearily.

"She looks like something from outer space!"

Harry nodded wearily.

Somehow, what with Josie, Harry, Fred, Astrid and Astrid's hair, there didn't seem to be much room in the kitchen. But gradually they all got settled. Astrid put the shepherd's pie on the table to cool.

"Now, Josie!" cried Astrid, eyes gleaming. "I want you to tell me about girls!"

Josie looked blank. "Girls?"

"Yes!" cried Astrid. "Girls! First I want to know what sort you are: silly or bossy?"

Josie gasped. "Silly or bossy?"

Astrid nodded. "All girls are one or the other! That's what Harry told me."

It was Harry's turn to gasp. "I never—" Then he stopped. Perhaps he had said something along those lines after a terrible school trip to the Natural History Museum. "Well, I didn't mean it like that!" he stammered. "I mean, you shouldn't . . ." He trailed off. He met Josie's gaze. Her eyes were narrowed.

"Harry Henderson!" she began. "How dare—" And then she broke off. With another gasp. The Smart Case was edging round the door. "What's that?" she shrieked.

Harry shrugged. "Oh . . . just a case," he said.

"It's Smarcase!" said Fred brightly. "Watch out – it'll bite your bum!"

Suddenly the Smart Case started moving faster over the floor. Towards Josie. She gave a piercing scream, and started scrambling onto the table for all the world as if she was escaping a huge metallic mouse.

Then everything happened at once. The table started to topple over. Astrid

grabbed at Josie to stop her falling.
Harry grabbed at the table to stop it
falling. But no-one grabbed the
shepherd's pie to stop it falling. There
was a CRASH!

Then all four of them were staring at
a horrible mess on the floor.

"Oh, dear!" said Harry.

This was bad. Losing the tea with any guest was bad enough. But losing the tea with Josie Phelps was a major disaster.

"Never mind!" said Astrid brightly. "We don't need shepherd's pie. I have something much nicer than that!"

At the mention of food, Josie seemed to recover a bit. Her eyes gleamed. "What?" she said hopefully.

Astrid smiled. "I've got ever so many dried bananas and—" She flung her arms out in triumph. "And swedes!"

"Well, she didn't stay very long," said Astrid.

Harry looked at his watch. "About eight minutes," he said.

"Disappointing," said Astrid sadly. "I didn't even get to ask her about the Brussels sprouts."

She knelt down to clear up the shepherd's pie. Her hair was beginning

to wilt. Harry got a cloth, and went
over to help her.

"It's OK," he said, mopping up some
spots of mince.

Astrid sighed. "OK?"

"Yes," said Harry. "I'll ask another
girl. I'll ask a girl called Sarah
Whitehouse."

## Chapter Fourteen

It was Thursday evening. Astrid was eating dried bananas. Fred was watching clips from *Mary Poppins*. Harry was hard at work, drawing a picture of outer space. He drew a planet with rings like Saturn, then another with three moons.

Harry looked up to see Mary Poppins clicking her fingers to tidy the kids' room. Yeah, that would be good, he thought. It would be fun to have a magic nanny. But let's face it, he thought with a grin, he and Fred had done better than those dopey kids in *Mary Poppins*. They might have had a magic nanny. But he and Fred had an au pair from outer space!

"Supercalifragilisticexpialidocious!" sang Mary Poppins.

Harry looked over at Astrid. She was leaning back in the chair, one hand holding the remote control, the other holding a piece of dried banana, her long hair falling down her back.

He turned back to his picture. He had
run out of ideas for planets now, so he
started doing a spaceship. It was a
silvery-green spaceship, speeding away
towards the unknown. Then he shaded
the background in dark blue and dotted
it with yellow pinpricks for stars.

He leaned back in his chair and stared at his finished picture. It was good. But something was wrong. Not with the picture, but with him. He wasn't feeling as happy as he should be. He should be happy.

It had been a good month. He had saved the house from imploding. He had sorted out Rod Beevor. And Sarah Whitehouse was coming to tea on Tuesday.

So what was it? Harry looked at the television, then at the picture – and then he knew. Mary Poppins left those kids at the end of the film, didn't she? And didn't the spaceship he had drawn speeding off into the galaxy look like Astrid's BCL-22?

His heart jumped. That was it! He had this funny feeling that Astrid was going to go soon. Perhaps even after Sarah had been to tea. Astrid might say she had got all she needed, and it was time for her to go . . . Suddenly he had to know. "Astrid," he said.

"Mmm?" said Astrid.

"Are you going soon? I mean – home, back to your own planet."

She nodded. "Yes, I suppose so. I thought I'd stay for one circuit."

He stared at her blankly "One circuit?"

"Yes, you know. One circuit of the Earth."

"You mean, one day!" Harry gasped. "Only one day more!"

"No, not one day," said Astrid. "One of those other things, you know. So you get all the seasons."

His heart leapt. "A year?"

Astrid nodded. "That's it. Fred's been telling me about the cold time, when you make snow-boys and put snow down people's backs. And also the hot time, when you go pink, if you're not careful, and there's a paggling pool in the park."

"Fed paggle wiv pants on!" said Fred happily.

She looked at him. "What do you think?"

"Me?" said Harry, his heart leaping. "I think that would be great! Great! I mean . . . there's lots more interesting stuff for you to see here." He met her green eyes. "And . . . and I'm so glad you're not about to go!"

She looked at him, and smiled. "Me, too, Harry," she said. "Me too . . ."

# The End

Professor Xn logged on to a report from one of his students. It was Project 492. He leant forward with interest. So here was Astrid's first report from Earth . . .

Soon he found himself plunged into a strange world of football, Coke, bikes, splitting trousers and prongs-for-eating-sweetcorn-on.

After a few minutes he paused, and scanned back to the section on "The Kitchen". There was a picture there — a metal object with a butterfly-shaped handle. He clicked his data-read. Lights flashed on the console, as the clear young voice rang out in the study. The words carried across the light years. The professor frowned, then repeated the words to himself.

"Fing what you open beans wiv . . ."

THE END

# THE DAD LIBRARY
## *Dennis Whelehan*
### *Illustrated by Tim Archbold*

*I wish you could change dads, the way you can change library books. I wish there was a Dad Library.*

Joseph is fed up with his dad. He forgets to go shopping, he cooks terrible meals, he doesn't help Joseph with his homework and he makes him eat school dinners.

Then Joseph discovers the Dad Library, crammed full with all sorts of wonderful dads. Should he borrow an Organizer Dad, or a Sporting Dad, or a Clever Dad, or an Indulgent Dad? Joseph wants to try them all. But which one will he want to keep?

ISBN 0 552 52979 6

Now available from all good book stores

YOUNG CORGI BOOKS

# THE DICK KING-SMITH COLLECTION
*Dick King-Smith*

E.S.P.
Eric Stanley Pigeon has a *very* unusual talent . . .

HORSE PIE
Three magnificent horses are in terrible danger . . .

THE GUARD DOG
A scruffy little mongrel has a big ambition – to be a guard dog . . .

Three wonderful animal stories from master storyteller Dick King-Smith, creator of *Babe*.

**'Dick King-Smith has brought magic into the lives of millions of children'**
*Parents*

ISBN 0 552 54610 0

Now available from all good book stores

YOUNG CORGI BOOKS